OVERCOMING ADVERSITY:
SHARING THE AMERICAN DREAM

TONY DUNGY

DISCARD

MASON CREST PUBLISHERS
PHILADELPHIA

OVERCOMING ADVERSITY:
SHARING THE AMERICAN DREAM

Charles Barkley	Norah Jones
Halle Berry	Martin Lawrence
Cesar Chavez	Bruce Lee
Kenny Chesney	Eva Longoria
George Clooney	Malcolm X
Johnny Depp	Carlos Mencia
Tony Dungy	Chuck Norris
Jermaine Dupri	Barack Obama
Jennifer Garner	Rosa Parks
Kevin Garnett	Bill Richardson
John B. Herrington	Russell Simmons
Salma Hayek	Carrie Underwood
Vanessa Hudgens	Modern American
Samuel L. Jackson	Indian Leaders

OVERCOMING ADVERSITY:
SHARING THE AMERICAN DREAM

TONY DUNGY

BRADY CARLISLE

MASON CREST PUBLISHERS
PHILADELPHIA

ABOUT CROSS-CURRENTS

When you see this logo, turn to the Cross-Currents section at the back of the book. The Cross-Currents features explore connections between people, places, events, and ideas.

Produced by OTTN Publishing, Stockton, New Jersey

Mason Crest Publishers
370 Reed Road
Broomall, PA 19008
www.masoncrest.com

First printing

1 3 5 7 9 8 6 4 2

Library of Congress Cataloging-in-Publication Data

Carlisle, Brady.
  Tony Dungy / Brady Carlisle.
      p. cm. — (Sharing the American dream : overcoming adversity)
  Includes bibliographical references and index.
  ISBN 978-1-4222-0588-4 (hc)
  ISBN 978-1-4222-0743-7 (pb)
  1. Dungy, Tony—Juvenile literature. 2. Football coaches—United States—Biography—Juvenile literature. 3. African American football coaches—Biography—Juvenile literature. I. Title.
  GV939.D84C37 2008
  796.332092—dc22
  [B]
                                        2008022992

OVERCOMING ADVERSITY:
SHARING THE AMERICAN DREAM

TABLE OF CONTENTS

CHAPTER ONE

GAINING THE WHOLE WORLD

On February 4, 2007, Tony Dungy, head coach of the Indianapolis Colts, stood on the sidelines of Dolphin Stadium in Miami, waiting for Super Bowl XLI to begin. On the other side of the field was his friend and former assistant coach, Lovie Smith, now the head coach of the Chicago Bears. One of them was about to become the first African-American coach to win the Super Bowl.

Competing in professional football's biggest game was not a new experience for Tony. As a reserve player with the 1978 Pittsburgh Steelers, he had achieved the dream of all young football players by winning a Super Bowl ring. But this particular game was different, because now he was a head coach. Several decades earlier, for an African American to even hold such a position seemed improbable.

Tony knew that merely appearing in the game with Smith would stir up strong feelings for many African Americans. In his memoir, *Quiet Strength,* Tony wrote that one of his daughter's college professors saw a strong connection between the coach's achievement and the civil rights demonstrations during the 1960s that opened doors for black people. "This is why we marched. . . . To see your dad standing up there," the professor told her.

Indianapolis head coach Tony Dungy (right) stands with his friend Lovie Smith, head coach of the Chicago Bears, during a press conference before Super Bowl XLI. The February 2007 championship game marked the first time that black Americans coached both Super Bowl teams.

Not everyone could appreciate the historical significance of this moment, as Tony was well aware. During the early years of his career, which now spanned 25 years, many obstacles stood in the way of Tony and other black coaches. As a young defensive coordinator for the Minnesota Vikings during the early 1990s, Tony had even received letters filled with racist, hateful words directed at him. During the thrilling moments of the Super Bowl, those enemies were in the back of his mind. However, true to his forgiving nature, he hoped that maybe some of those people had changed their minds.

READ MORE

For some history about the Super Bowl, read "The Big Game" on page 44.

A Different Kind of Coach

Over the course of his distinguished career, Tony has sought to change the way people think NFL coaches should conduct themselves. Tony has always been calm and quiet. He has never embarrassed his players. He hasn't treated losses as if they were the end of the world.

He believes that as long as players concentrate on doing the little things right, avoiding mistakes, and playing as hard as they can, in the end they can win. Furthermore, he believes that players and coaches should keep a healthy perspective on what is most important. They should put family, faith, and community first.

According to Tony, players and coaches should have another life outside of the game. While some coaches brag about spending 15 hours a day at the stadium, where they lead practices and study film, Tony believes it matters more to spend time at home and be involved in activities away from the football field.

Tony reacts to a play while coaching the Tampa Bay Buccaneers during a January 2002 playoff game. Although Tony had been a successful NFL head coach for more than a decade, he was criticized when his teams came up short in the playoffs. Before Super Bowl XLI, some people felt Tony would never be able to win a championship.

Priorities

Throughout Tony's career, however, it has been hard to prove that such an approach is the right one. In football, as with all professional sports, the priority is to win championships. Although in Tony's previous stint as head coach of the Tampa Bay Buccaneers he had set a positive example *and* had improved the team's record, he had never gotten them to the Super Bowl. For falling short of that ultimate goal, he was fired in 2002.

To make matters worse, Tony's successor, Jon Gruden, brought the Buccaneers to the

READ MORE

Read "African-American Coaches in the NFL" to learn how the league has tried to promote the hiring of qualified blacks as head coaches. Go to page 45.

Super Bowl and won the following season. Gruden was not a mild-tempered coach like Tony was; he was an emotional, fire-breathing leader who did not hesitate to put in long hours at the stadium. For many observers, the Buccaneers' success under Gruden answered the question about what an NFL coach should be like. A "nice guy" like Tony Dungy might be able to improve a franchise and teach players to play well, but he didn't have what it took to lead them to victory. He couldn't "fire up" his players for the big games, they said.

After a few years as coach at Indianapolis, the same whispers about Tony's limitations grew louder. Tony had made the Colts consistent winners throughout the regular seasons, but again and again he had failed to steer them through the playoffs to the Super Bowl.

Despite the criticisms against him, Tony believed in his way. He understands that football is important to many people, but it isn't life's biggest priority. Coming from a family of health professionals and educators, he is quick to recognize their contributions over his own. "My line of work gives me more notoriety in some circles," Tony wrote in his memoir, "but they're all doing things that are much more important in the long run."

Super Bowl XLI was special. But in the days leading up to the game, Tony wrote in his memoir, he thought often about a bible verse, Matthew 16:26, in which Jesus asks, "And what do you benefit if you gain the whole world but lose your own soul?" Victory would not matter if Tony's players didn't do things the right way—the way he believed they should. Tony wanted his team to win without sacrificing its values or priorities.

CHAPTER TWO

LEARNING COMPOSURE

Tony Dungy's parents had high expectations for their son, who was born on October 6, 1955. They knew that many of Tony's peers growing up in Jackson, Michigan, expected to find jobs in a local factory after finishing high school. After all, the small town of Jackson, located near Detroit and East Lansing, generally revolved around the automobile industry.

Tony's parents, however, were both teachers. They expected their son and his three siblings to go to college. And they hoped for the same future for many of their own students.

Tony remembers his mother, CleoMae, teaching her students the importance of studying and a love of sports. CleoMae Dungy had been an accomplished basketball player as a young girl in her native Ontario, Canada. In addition to teaching

CleoMae Dungy, Tony's mother, was a respected English teacher and cheerleading coach in Jackson, Michigan. In 2002, the library at Frost Elementary School in Jackson was named in her honor.

Tony's father, Wilbur Dungy, watches his son direct the team during a Tampa Bay practice in 1996.

English at Jackson High School, she also coached the school's cheerleading squad. Often, if her children had finished their homework and behaved, she would offer them the treat of riding on one of the team's buses to Jackson's away games.

Wilbur Dungy also demonstrated a love for both academics and sports. A physiology professor at Jackson Community College, he competed in boxing and track and field in his younger days. He also had the distinction of being one of the Tuskegee Airmen, the nation's first African-American fighter pilots who achieved high honors during World War II.

However, Wilbur was a quiet man and never talked to Tony about that phase in his life. In fact, Tony didn't learn about his dad's achievements with the Tuskegee Airmen until Wilbur's funeral in 2004. Tony remembers most his father's love for fishing and how he would use family time out on the lake to teach his children an appreciation of nature.

Tony learned a lot from his parents, but their greatest lessons were about how to treat others. Through their examples as teachers,

READ MORE

Read "The War Heroes from Tuskegee" to learn more about the Tuskegee Airmen. Go to page 46.

he learned how to tap into the potential of learners who most needed encouragement. He watched his parents work just as hard to motivate the struggling students as they did with the star pupils. In his memoir, Tony remembers his father telling him, "If you're going to be a good teacher, you can't just teach the A students. A good teacher is one who helps everybody earn an A."

Tony has often applied his parents' lessons to coaching. He has told his assistants that they have to help all their players to play their best. But there are different ways to help players achieve great results, because as his father taught him, a teaching approach that works for one individual might not work for another. Everyone learns differently, whether it entails learning a new offensive scheme or mastering a science lesson.

Sports Star

From 1963 to 1966, the Dungy family lived on the campus of Michigan State University while Wilbur worked to obtain his physiology degree. During this time, Tony grew to love college football. With its renowned football program, Michigan State provided great exposure to the game. Tony dreamed of playing at Michigan State someday. Football wasn't his only interest, though. He loved playing basketball as well.

Tony's athletic skills were apparent at a young age. When he was 14 years old, he was mentioned in the "Faces in the Crowd" column of *Sports Illustrated,* a regular feature that highlighted student athletes. The blurb read:

> Tony Dungy, 14, student president of Frost Junior High in Jackson, Mich., threw 23 touchdown passes over the past three seasons, is high scorer in basketball for the third straight year and has never

been defeated in high and low hurdles and long jump in track.

Dealing With a Hot Temper

Along with demonstrating great talent, Tony gained a reputation as a hothead. During one particular basketball game in ninth grade, he was thrown out for fighting. He had become irate that an opposing player kept hacking him but was not getting called for the fouls. He complained to the referee, but received no help from him. Feeling he had no recourse, Tony swung at the other player, knocking him down. The offense resulted in Tony's ejection from the game.

As Tony expected, his father stepped forward to offer an important lesson about the scuffle on the court. "What did you accomplish? Do you think you helped your team in the locker room?" his father asked him. Tony recalled his own response to those questions to *USA Today*: "I thought about it and said, 'No. I got my emotions out, but I didn't help my team.' My dad had always told me . . . composure was more important than emotion. I think I finally learned that and really changed when I got to pro football."

There were more lessons for Tony to learn after he landed the quarterback spot on his high school football team. At the end of his junior year, he found out that he had been made a team captain for the upcoming football season. He also learned that his best friend, who was an excellent wide receiver and like Tony was black, had not been named a captain. Tony suspected racism was behind the decision to pick only one African-American captain.

In protest, Tony quit the team. Responding to his son's decision, Wilbur stopped short of telling him to rejoin the squad, but he did ask Tony to think about how quitting was going to make the situation better. Tony didn't care. He was just angry.

A school counselor and longtime friend, Leroy Rocquemore, suggested a course of action even harder for Tony to accept. Rocquemore advised Tony to go back to the team. He warned him that by refusing to play, he was denying himself the opportunity to do something at which he could really excel. He added that in the end, Tony was just hurting himself and the rest of the team.

Tony agreed to return to the team but was angered when the coach said that he had to make amends, which including doing extra running drills and washing dishes at training camp. Looking to appease Tony, Rocquemore explained that the coach was the coach and Tony was the player. In other words, sometimes you have to do some things in life you don't want to do.

Tony accepted the coach's conditions and returned to the team. Eventually, he realized that the coach and Mr. Rocquemore had been right. He learned that he had to be careful not to make snap judgments and impulsive decisions. During an enjoyable senior year, Tony repaired his relationship with his coach. In his memoir, he reported that the two of them still remain close.

Minnesota

Tony had always thought he would play football at Michigan State University, where he had first become familiar with the game. He particularly admired the team's coach, Duffy Daugherty. However, when Tony learned that Coach Daugherty was going to retire, he began considering other schools.

Tony finally decided to attend the University of Minnesota, where he could play basketball as well as football. He liked the city of Minneapolis as well as the university's coaches. What struck Tony was how Minnesota's head football coach, Cal Stoll, handled his staff. He hired assistants he trusted and who he

Tony attended the University of Minnesota in Minneapolis, pictured above, from 1973 to 1977. As the football team's starting quarterback, Tony led the Golden Gophers to winning seasons in his junior and senior years. He also excelled in the classroom, earning Academic All–Big Ten honors.

knew could teach the players. One of these assistants, quarterbacks coach Tom Moore, even became a lasting friend of Tony's who would help him out a number of times in later years.

Tony was injured during his sophomore season, and this convinced him to quit the basketball team. He continued to excel on the football field, however. By the time he graduated in 1977 with a degree in business administration, he held a number of school records, including pass attempts (576), completions (274), passing yards (3,577), and touchdown passes (25). He was twice named the team's

READ MORE

To learn about some African Americans who succeeded as quarterbacks in the NFL, read "Pioneer Quarterbacks" on page 47.

Most Valuable Player. With that kind of résumé, he expected to win a professional contract through the NFL draft.

Disappointment

When Tony's name was not called on draft day, he was shocked. Other players from the Minnesota team were drafted, including Tony's roommate. It was devastating to learn that no team seemed to want him. Most people told Tony that he hadn't been drafted because at only six foot one, he was too small. He also had a quarterback style based on running and scrambling to move his team forward, which did not appeal to most coaches. At that time, pro teams preferred strong-armed quarterbacks who would drop back and pass down the field.

However, there was still an open door for Tony. After the NFL draft, it is typical for teams to contact players who didn't get drafted but who show potential. Organizations will send out invitations for players to attend their training camps, where they hold tryouts for the remaining positions on their rosters. Tony received a few invitations. Instead of offering him a chance to play quarterback, however, he was asked to try out as a defensive back or wide receiver. It was still a chance to play in the NFL, but Tony was not sure about switching positions.

Although Tony received no attractive offers from the NFL, a Canadian Football League team did approach him, offering him a $50,000 bonus to play quarterback. (At the time, this was a lot of money, although it is a small sum by today's standards). But Tony decided he wanted to play in the NFL, not in Canada. He began considering an offer from the Buffalo Bills to play as a free safety.

A Welcome Call

One day, as Tony was mulling over his options, he received a phone call from an old friend from the University of Minnesota.

Coach Tom Moore believed that Tony could play in the NFL, and encouraged him to attend Pittsburgh's training camp in 1977.

It was Tom Moore, who since leaving Minnesota had taken a job coaching wide receivers for the Pittsburgh Steelers. He had recently talked about Tony's potential with the Steelers' head coach, Chuck Noll. Pittsburgh wanted Tony to come to its training camp.

Tony thoughtfully considered the pros and cons of playing, should he make the team. While there was no chance he would play quarterback, he was excited because the Steelers were a veteran team. This fact aroused his interest because he knew that since there was little pressure on established players to show their abilities during training camp, Tony had a much better chance to impress the coaches.

Another incentive to take the offer was that the Steelers were one of the NFL's best teams. Pittsburgh had won the Super Bowl in 1974 and 1975. Also, the team had a large, dedicated group of fans, and the Rooney family, which owned the Steelers, cared deeply about the team. It was clear that the pros outweighed the cons. Tony decided to take Moore's offer and go to Pittsburgh.

CHAPTER THREE

DIFFERENT ROADS

Tony Dungy came to the Steelers training camp eager to play. The only problem was that the team did not know exactly *where* he would play. The original plan was for Tony to play as wide receiver, but with injuries to a number of other players, the coaches needed to fill a gap in the defense. After some discussion, they moved Tony to safety.

After years of playing quarterback, Tony discovered that he really enjoyed learning these different positions. He also could count on new mentors to help him out. Veteran players such as Mel Blount, Jimmy Allen, and Donnie Shell showed him the ropes.

Tony Dungy on the sidelines of a Pittsburgh Steelers game during his rookie season, 1977.

Working with defensive coordinator Bud Carson gave Tony a chance to learn from one of the geniuses of the game.

Tony was intrigued by his new defensive teammates. These players were often considered the fiercest competitors on the field. Away from the game, though, they were kind, thoughtful men of faith. Their personalities flew in the face of the notion that a football player had to be tough and mean. Tony learned that he could be a hard-hitting fighter during a game but a gentle person off the field.

Learning to Win

Tony also admired his new head coach, Chuck Noll. In one of the first training sessions, Noll told the players what would make them winners:

> Champions don't beat themselves. If you want to win, do the ordinary things better than anyone else does—day in and day out. We're not going to fool people or outscheme them. We're just going to outplay them. Because we'll know what we're doing. When we get into a critical situation, we won't have to think. We'll play fast and fundamentally sound.

Tony counted himself lucky to be with great teammates and coaches. He was eager to take the new position at safety. Early on, however, he was surprised to discover that his quarterback days weren't quite over. The Steelers needed an emergency quarterback,

READ MORE

To find out more about legendary NFL coach Chuck Noll, read "A Champion Coach." Go to page 48.

Tony (number 21) intercepts a pass during a 1978 game against the Buffalo Bills. Even though Tony was a reserve defensive back, he led the team in interceptions during the 1978 season, with six. He also recovered two fumbles during the season.

a role normally filled by someone who plays a different position. (The emergency quarterback is only called in if the team's three quarterbacks on the roster become injured.)

In a game during Tony's rookie season, the Steelers found themselves with their starting quarterback, Terry Bradshaw, and his backup, Mike Kruczek, both injured. At the time, the team's third quarterback was on the inactive list. With no other quarterback available, Noll sent in Tony to finish the game.

It was a disaster. Tony fumbled a snap, botched a handoff, and threw two interceptions. The Steelers lost, 27–10. However, Tony pulled off a rare feat that day—he intercepted a pass and threw an interception in the same game!

Tony got over the embarrassment, and had the fortune of being able to play in the playoffs as a rookie. The Steelers failed to advance past the first round, however. Then, as Tony's second season approached, he was dismayed when he came down with an illness. However, his health bounced back and he had a great year, leading the team in interceptions.

The Steelers turned in a much better performance during the 1978 playoffs and made the Super Bowl. Then, to cap off what Tony calls a "miracle year," they defeated the Dallas Cowboys in Super Bowl XIII, 35–31. Ironically, the glory of winning the Super Bowl did not dramatically change Tony's perspective on things. "Despite all the good things that occurred that year," he wrote in his memoir, "I can still look back and say that 1978 was the first season in my life in which sports weren't the most important thing to me."

Moving On

Tony's levelheaded perspective would prove valuable as his third NFL season approached. As the Steelers training camp came to an end, he realized that one final cut remained, and that he could be the player who had to go. Many of the other defensive players were stars, and he was just a backup. Tony's suspicions were confirmed when he received word that he had been traded to another team, the San Francisco 49ers.

The 49ers were a struggling team with a new coach, Bill Walsh, and a rookie quarterback, Joe Montana. Although those two men would go on to lead some of the greatest squads in NFL history, when Tony joined the 49ers in 1979 the team was still a few seasons away from reaching its true potential.

The 49ers finished the 1979 season with only two wins. Then, after only one year with the team, Tony was traded to the

New York Giants. More bad news came as the training camp neared its final days in 1980—he was cut from the team.

Making the Next Move

Getting the axe from the Giants was tough for Tony to handle. He was uncertain about his next move. After he had been traded a few times and then finally cut, it appeared his career as a player in the NFL was likely over.

As one point while considering another path, he remembered that during his short time with the Giants, head coach Ray Perkins had offered him some helpful words of advice. Observing that Tony was smart and worked hard, Perkins told him that he might make a good coach someday.

Tony went back to the University of Minnesota to work out and stay ready if another team called. Heeding Perkins' advice, he also volunteered as a coach for the university's team to see if the job suited him.

After the 1980 season ended, Perkins offered Tony a coaching job. When this news got back to the Steelers, the organization made its own offer to Tony. As he considered the decision, he recalled how he had loved playing for the Steelers. He decided to return to Pittsburgh as an assistant coach. At age 25, he became the youngest assistant coach in the NFL.

Just like Tony had remembered as a rookie player, Pittsburgh offered plenty of learning opportunities. Chuck Noll,

In 1981, the Steelers hired Tony to coach the team's defensive backs. At age 25, Tony became the NFL's youngest assistant coach.

who was still the team's head coach, continued to show him how to live a balanced life with an NFL career. Noll told his players and coaches, "Football is what you are doing right now, but it's not your life's work. You've got to continue to prepare for your life's work." Tony was reminded that it was okay to have a life outside of football. Someone could be a great coach without living in his office. He could have hobbies, other interests, and even a family.

A New Life

It was a simple message, but one that needed to reach Tony, who was putting in long hours as a new coach. He needed to be reminded that he was young and single and should be meeting people. After much prodding from a pastor at a local church, he reluctantly agreed to meet a girl who the pastor thought was perfect for him.

Immediately, Tony knew the pastor was right—Lauren Harris was different than other girls he had met. They began to see each other and before the end of the year, Tony proposed. They were married on June 19, 1982.

The next few years brought more good fortune for Tony in his career and personal life. He continued to ascend the Steelers' coaching ranks by becoming a defensive coordinator. That same year, he also became a father when Lauren gave birth to a daughter, Tiara. Then, in 1987, they had a son, James.

Leaving Pittsburgh

The Steelers had a poor season in 1988. The team's dismal performance left Noll under pressure to make changes to his coaching staff. One change he pursued was asking Tony to step down from his coordinator position and become coach of the defensive backs.

Tony and Lauren Dungy with their family, 1997. From left to right are Tiara, Lauren, James, Eric, and Tony.

Rather than accept a demotion, Tony decided it would be better to take a job with another team. He resigned and became the defensive backs coach in Kansas City, where he stayed for three seasons. Then, in 1992, the Minnesota Vikings offered Tony a more attractive position as defensive coordinator. The Dungy family, who now included baby Eric, picked up and moved once more.

In Minnesota, Tony loved working with head coach Dennis Green. He was a "chief executive" type of coach, like Chuck Noll and Tony's college coach, Cal Stoll. Green hired assistants he trusted and let them do

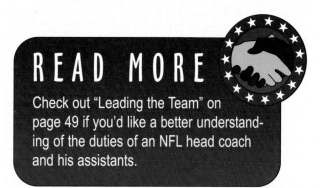

READ MORE

Check out "Leading the Team" on page 49 if you'd like a better understanding of the duties of an NFL head coach and his assistants.

their job. He was also interested in developing the careers of his assistants. Rather than forbidding them to speak to the media as some coaches did, he let them speak freely. He asked them for their ideas when it came to important decisions. Finally, Green highly valued family. He gave coaches days off to spend at home and encouraged them to bring their families to training camp.

Building Defenses

During his years in Minnesota, Tony's defenses were some of the best in the NFL. In his first year with the team, Tony worked with a squad of young players that finished the season ranked eighth overall in the NFL. The team improved to have the number one defense in the league in 1993. Minnesota retained a solid defense the following year.

The successful seasons with Minnesota gained Tony a reputation as a top defensive coordinator. He had his sights on getting a head coaching job, although few interviews for such positions were forthcoming. After the 1995 season, however, he was presented a chance when the Tampa Bay Buccaneers called him for a meeting.

At first, Tony doubted he would get the Tampa Bay job. There were more well-known candidates who were being considered, and he thought he hadn't made a good impression on the general manager who interviewed him. But he was wrong. In 1996, Tony was hired as head coach of the Tampa Bay Buccaneers.

CHAPTER FOUR

IN CONTROL

The day he had awaited was finally here: Tony was now head coach of an NFL team. The only problem was that when he arrived in 1996, the Tampa Bay Buccaneers were struggling as a team. Their last winning season had been in 1982.

Tony had to change the losing culture that plagued the team. He turned his focus on the coaching staff. His plan, which he described in *Quiet Strength,* was to put together a group of coaches who were "teachers more than tacticians, smart coaches who were driven to accomplish our goals and could get those goals across."

Tony also discovered that the team's facilities, like the coaching staff, were in need of a makeover. The Bucs' headquarters, known as One Buccaneer Place, had no adjacent parking lot, and its staff meeting rooms doubled as offices. Making matters worse was the location of One Buccaneer Place—right near the runways of Tampa Bay International Airport. The roar of jet airplanes taking off or landing could be deafening.

No Excuses

Tony resisted any temptation to blame Tampa's recent spate of losses on the rundown facilities. Instead, he remembered what his father had told him about teaching in the days of segregation, when African-American children learned in separate schools that were often strapped for resources. Wilbur stressed that "it didn't matter what his building looking like; his job was to help his students learn just as much as the students in the other building were learning." Tony told his players not to look for things they could use as excuses for losing. Instead they should focus on playing smart and doing the little things right.

Despite the new faces and high hopes, the team got off to a bad start in 1996. Tampa Bay lost its first five games, three of which were blowouts. Few fans came to the games, and those that did show up openly showed their frustration with the team. The Glazer family, owners of the Bucs, reassured Tony that he had their support and that they would be patient while the team rebuilt. Tony's former coach, Chuck Noll, also offered encouragement. He reminded Tony that he had lost 13 of 14 games in his first year as Pittsburgh's head coach.

Players expected Tony to be angry about the losses, but he remained calm. Ironically, his single blow-up during the whole season stemmed from a concern that had nothing to do with football. He became irate when he learned that one player had been late to an autograph session and another had completely missed an appearance at a local grammar school. Tony told the team that being accountable off the field was just as important as being accountable on it. He expected his players to give 100 percent in everything they did and to understand that it really mattered that they fulfill all their commitments.

Eventually, the team began fulfilling its commitment to win. The Bucs won five of their last seven games in 1996 to finish with a 6–10 record. To the general public it may have seemed like just another losing season for Tampa Bay, but for those paying close attention, it was easy to sense change. Under Tony's leadership, the team was beginning to believe it could win.

Getting Better

The Buccaneers got off to a 5–0 start in 1997 and finished with a 10–6 record. They made the playoffs for the first time in 15 years. Tampa Bay won its first playoff game, against Detroit, but lost in the second round to the previous year's Super Bowl champs, the Green Bay Packers. Still, there was a great deal of excitement around the improved team and the developments its new coach had put in place.

In spite of the fans' high hopes, 1998 turned out to be a frustrating year. Tony felt the players did not realize their true potential.

Tony shakes hands with Tampa Bay owner Malcolm Glazer after being introduced as the Buccaneers head coach, January 22, 1996. He took over an awful team: between 1983 and 1995, the Bucs won just 58 games and lost 150, for a woeful .279 winning percentage.

Failing to heed Tony's words about playing smart and focusing on the little things, the Bucs made too many mistakes on the field. They finished with a lackluster 8–8 record, and as a result they missed the playoffs.

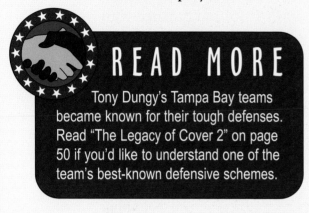

READ MORE

Tony Dungy's Tampa Bay teams became known for their tough defenses. Read "The Legacy of Cover 2" on page 50 if you'd like to understand one of the team's best-known defensive schemes.

In 1999, a successful draft offered promise of a better season. However, the team got off to an ugly 3–4 start. They were struggling to score points, as Tony labored to find a quarterback who could properly lead the offense. Starting quarterback Trent Dilfer rebounded from a poor performance in the first seven games to lead the team on a three-game winning streak. Then, just as things were improving, Dilfer was injured.

Tony decided to put rookie Shaun King in as the starting quarterback and the team won three more games. In a few weeks, the Bucs had become a 9–4 team with a chance to finish first in their conference. Safety John Lynch gave Tony the credit for the Bucs' dramatic turnaround, telling a *New York Times* reporter:

> A lot of times you take on the personality of your leader. Rather than complicate things, Coach simplified things, emphasizing what we do well. When you see the leader not panic and just chip away at being successful, you follow that.

The team finished the year 11–5, winning the conference and earning a first-round bye. They beat the Washington Redskins, 14–13, in their first playoff game, then played the

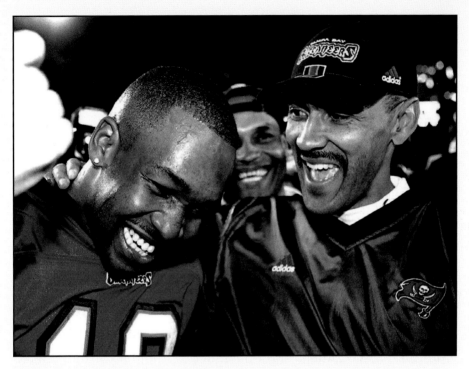

Tony's belief in rookie quarterback Shaun King paid off, as the team won the National Football Conference (NFC) Central Division in 1999 with an 11–5 record. Here, Dungy and King celebrate after Tampa Bay's first-round playoff victory over the Redskins.

St. Louis Rams for the conference championship and a shot to go to the Super Bowl. The game came down to the wire, but the Rams proved too powerful and the Bucs lost, 11–6.

A Disappointing End

The Bucs continued to make the playoffs, reaching the post-season in both 2000 and 2001. However, Tampa Bay was quickly eliminated both years. Tony could see that attitudes about the team had changed again. Although everyone praised Tampa Bay's defense, fans began to complain that the team was not scoring enough. After a playoff loss that ended the 2001 season, the Bucs' owners decided it was time to make a change. They fired Tony.

Tony was disappointed by the news. The Dungy family had established strong roots in Tampa. Tony and Lauren had expanded their family by adopting two children—a baby boy, Jordan, in 2000, and a girl, Jade, in 2001.

Tony and his wife had also grown attached to Tampa through the many service endeavors they pursued. Lauren volunteered for different community groups. Tony had been involved in starting an organization called All Pro Dad that taught men how to become better fathers. He had also founded Mentors for Life, a group that gave tickets to Bucs games to local children and their mentors. While juggling all these commitments he had managed time for a prison ministry, through which he visited inmates to talk to them both about football and faith. This last area of service particularly sparked Tony's interest. After he was fired by the Bucs, he even considered leaving football and pursuing prison ministry full-time.

Indianapolis

A timely call from Jim Irsay, the owner of the Indianapolis Colts, helped change Tony's mind. Irsay wanted Tony as his team's new head coach. Irsay's interest was not solely based on the coach's ability to get the Colts more wins. He also saw Tony as someone who could instill strong values in the organization and make it a visible presence in the Indianapolis community. Although Tony had also received an invitation to coach from the Carolina Panthers, he chose the Colts, drawn to Irsay's community-focused mission.

The Colts were a veteran team with a powerful offense. But they also suffered from a weak defense. It was clear Tony would have to devote a lot of time to the Colts' defensive game. His new focus was a source of concern for some of the Colts, including star quarterback Peyton Manning. The fear was that by making the defense a priority, Tony would neglect the offense. The players had no desire to see their high-flying offense turn into a low-scoring unit like the Bucs' offense.

Tony asked Manning to trust him. He explained that a good defense would take some of the burden off the quarterback and the rest of the offense. Tony shared with the *New York Times* his thoughts about Manning as they prepared for the 2002 season:

> It's going to be good for him to know that we don't expect him to win the games by himself. We expect him to win a lot for us, but everybody is going to have to pull their weight and do it. We don't expect him to be Superman.

A Good Start

Tony kept his word. He let Manning and the talented offense, including wide receiver Marvin Harrison and running back Edgerrin James, lead the way. Meanwhile, he drafted a new group of defensive players and quickly taught them the Colts' strategy.

The Colts made the play-offs in their first year under Tony, but lost in the first round to the New York Jets. In 2003, the team went 12–4, but lost to the New England Patriots in the American Football Conference (AFC) championship game.

READ MORE

To learn more about Colts star Peyton Manning, his brother Eli, and their father Archie, read "A Family of Quarterbacks" on page 51.

The Colts went 12–4 again in 2004, as the offense had another successful year. Manning even set a new NFL record for most touchdown passes in a single season. In the divisional

Colts quarterback Peyton Manning listens to Tony's instructions on the sidelines during a 2003 game. When Tony arrived in Indianapolis, his friend and former mentor Tom Moore had been working as the Colts' offensive coordinator since 1998. Moore had built a high-scoring unit, so Tony was able to focus on improving the team's defense.

round of the playoffs, the Colts again took on the Patriots. Tony and his team faced their rivals with confidence, but the offense did not produce and the Patriots won, 20–3. It was the sixth time in Tony's coaching career that he had reached the playoffs but failed to make it to the Super Bowl.

Going into the 2005 season, many people began wondering if Tony's defense would ever come together, or if the Indianapolis offense could in fact rise to the occasion when it really mattered. But many fears were put to rest after the Colts won their first 13 games in 2005. They even beat their rivals, the Patriots.

Indianapolis fans began to talk not only about the playoffs and the Super Bowl, but about whether the team could go undefeated. During that streak fans also celebrated a career landmark for Tony: he became the 35th coach in NFL history to earn 100 career victories. The Colts finally lost in week 14, but as they prepared once again for the playoffs, no one could deny that Tony had led his team through a special season.

CHAPTER FIVE

KEEPING YOUR SOUL

When Tony had taken the Colts job, his family faced a new challenge—having two homes in different cities. Lauren and the children had remained in Tampa for a period so that Tiara, the oldest daughter, could continue going to her school. Spending time together remained a family priority. Lauren and the children helped make it work by regularly flying to games on weekends and visiting Tony during vacations. Tony's sons, James (nicknamed "Jamie") and Eric, were often found in the Colts' offices and on the sidelines during games.

Being separated from his family for long spells was difficult for Tony, so he was relieved when in 2005 his whole family gathered in Indianapolis for the Thanksgiving holiday. However, with many guests visiting that day, Tony only was able to say a quick goodbye to Tiara and Jamie as they rushed out to the door. They were headed to the airport, where they would take returning flights to their respective colleges. Tiara was going back to Spelman College in Atlanta, Georgia; Jamie was returning to Hillsborough Community College in Tampa.

That day was the last time Tony saw his oldest son. Early in the morning of December 22, 2005, the Dungys received a

James "Jamie" Dungy, wearing a grey shirt, stands on the Colts sideline during a 2004 game. In December 2005, the Dungy family suffered a devastating loss when 18-year-old Jamie committed suicide.

phone call from a hospital in Tampa. Jamie had committed suicide. He was just a few weeks away from his 19th birthday.

A Strong Show of Support

The entire Colts organization—players, coaches, and executives—flew to Tampa for Jamie's funeral. Members of the Bucs who had worked with Tony also attended. Three head coaches who were close with Tony—Herm Edwards, Lovie Smith, and Denny Green—also took time off from their coaching responsibilities to attend. Many other friends from the Dungys' Tampa days were there.

Tony spoke at the funeral. He talked about how it was

READ MORE

Read "A Tragic Problem" to learn more about suicide among young people. Go to page 52.

important at a time like this to try to find joy. He reminded the people gathered what a good person Jamie had been, about how kind he was to everyone and how loyal he was to his friends. Tony also talked about how difficult it was to be a teenager. Teens receive a lot of mixed messages, he explained, and they find it hard to take advice from adults, particularly their parents.

Attempting to find a lesson in the tragedy, Tony shared words of wisdom with the parents and kids there:

> Parents, hug your kids—every chance you get. Tell them that you love them every chance you get. You don't know when it's going to be the last time. . . . And for you kids—I know there are a number of you here today who are thirteen, fourteen, fifteen—maybe your parents are starting to seem a little old-fashioned, and maybe they won't let you do some of the things you want to do. Just know, when that happens, that they still love you and care about you very much. And those old-fashioned things will start making sense pretty soon.

He also talked to the football players in attendance and urged them to be good role models. He said:

> Continue being who you are, because our young people today need to hear from you. If anything, be bolder in who you are, because our boys are getting a lot of wrong messages today about what it means to be a man in this world, about how they should act and talk and dress and treat people. They aren't always getting the right message, but

you guys have the right message, and you live it, and we need you to continue to do that.

When the Dungys left the church to go to the cemetery, cars full of people who had been expecting the procession pulled over by the side of the road. People waved, holding up signs that wished the family well. The Dungys had not been forgotten in Tampa.

After Jamie

The Dungys relied on their faith to get them through the hard times after Jamie's death. They heard from many people, both friends and strangers, who offered their condolences. They also received support from many individuals whose own families had been touched by suicide.

As the Dungys tried to cope with Jamie's sudden death, many people who didn't know Tony personally offered messages of support.

After several days of mourning, Tony resumed his life as coach. Although the Irsays had told him to take as much time away as he wanted, he returned in time for the last game of the season. They beat the Arizona Cardinals, and the celebration that followed was emotional for Tony as well as the players, who were eager to claim a victory for their bereaved coach.

The team headed into the playoffs as heavy favorites. Their first contest was against the Pittsburgh Steelers. As much as the Colts wanted to deliver more wins for their grieving coach, they could not overcome the Steelers and lost, 21–18. The Colts' season came to a sudden end.

During the off-season, the Dungys continued to work through their grief about Jamie. They also made two huge decisions. One, Tony confirmed that he would coach the Colts the next season, in spite of the emotional burden he still felt from Jamie's death. Two, he and Lauren decided to adopt a baby boy, Justin.

Dealing with Doubts

A general feeling of uncertainty about the Colts marked the beginning of the 2006 season. Several players had left for other teams, and fans were anxious if the new players could deliver. People were also beginning to wonder about Tony and his team's playoff failures. They wondered if the "window of opportunity" for the Colts' star players might be closing.

Unfazed by the fans' doubts, Tony continued to believe in his way of doing things. He felt if the team just played the right way and always did their best, their time would come. They would make it through the playoffs and into the Super Bowl.

The Colts started 2006 with nine straight wins, and they finished with a 12–4 record and made the playoffs. It was no surprise that Tony had brought his team to the playoffs once again. However, this time the Colts weren't the favorites, as they had been in previous seasons.

Moving Through the Playoffs

The Colts advanced through the first round of playoffs by blowing by the Kansas City Chiefs. In their next game against the Baltimore Ravens, the Colts won again by allowing only six points. Now the team was only one game away from the Super Bowl. However, to get there, they would have to beat the New

England Patriots, the team that had eliminated the Colts two times in their last three playoff appearances.

The Colts had a poor start against the Patriots, going into halftime behind with the score 21 to 6. During the halftime break, Tony reminded his team that they had been down by 21 points against the Patriots in 2003 and almost had come all the way back to win. A 15-point lead could be overcome.

It seems Tony's words gave the Colts the confidence they needed. They rallied to tie the game, and by the two-minute mark in the fourth quarter, they were trailing by only three points, with the score 34–31. Manning led the team down the field and the Colts scored a touchdown to take the lead. The

The Indianapolis defense moves to break up a running play during a 2006 victory over the Philadelphia Eagles. That season, the team's defense was not as good as it had been in 2005. However, the Colts were able to stop opponents when it counted—in the NFL playoffs.

Patriots then made a last-minute attempt to reclaim the lead, but a Colts' interception ended the game. Tony and the team were headed to Miami, Florida, to play against the Chicago Bears in Super Bowl XLI.

An Historic Super Bowl

The thought of playing in the Super Bowl was exciting, but for Tony, winning a conference championship after so many playoff losses felt just as good. Still, the big game against the

READ MORE

If you'd like to learn a little about the coaches who influenced Tony, and those who have been influenced by him, read "A Rich Coaching Heritage." Go to page 53.

Chicago Bears, led by Lovie Smith, was historic. Either Tony or Smith would become the first African-American head coach to win the championship game.

Tony searched for the right words of inspiration. The night before the game, he told his team:

> Tomorrow night, there is going to be a storm in Dolphin Stadium. We might get off to a slow start and have to claw our way back, but we can do it. We will do it. Do what we do. Don't panic. Stay the course.

The next day there *was* a storm—it rained all day in Miami, and it continued throughout the game. The Bears got off to a fast start when Devin Hester returned the opening kickoff for a touchdown. The Colts pulled ahead, though, and led the game at halftime, 16–14.

During the second half, Tony proudly watched his team perform just the way he had taught them—by playing smart and doing the little things right. All of the hard work paid off,

Tony holds the Lombardi Trophy after the Colts won Super Bowl XLI.

as the game ended with a 29–17 Colts victory.

Tony later wrote that as the final minute of the game ticked away, he thought about all the important people in his life— friends, the coaches he'd learned from, players he'd worked with, and Jim Irsay, the Colts owner who'd trusted him when others did not. And as he ascended the platform to receive the Super Bowl trophy, Tony thought about his family, including the missing members: his mother, who had died in 2002; his father, who had died in 2004; and Jamie.

Moving On

After winning the Super Bowl, Tony decided to write a memoir, *Quiet Strength.* The book offers readers Tony's testimony about life, coaching, and the importance of faith. It spent two weeks at number one on the *New York Times* nonfiction bestseller list. For 15 consecutive weeks it remained among that list's top 15 books. Over a million copies of the book are in print, making it one of the best-selling sports-related books in history. Following the success of *Quiet Strength,* Tony published another title, the motivational children's book *You Can Do It!*

In contrast to the Colts' championship season in 2006, the follow-up season was injury-filled and difficult. The team made it to the playoffs, but lost in the first round. Afterwards, many people wondered if Tony would return. He took some time off to think about it, but finally announced he would coach again in 2008. The Colts' owners and the players were relieved when they heard that they would have Tony at the helm for at least another season.

Throughout Tony Dungy's career, people have questioned his ideas about coaching. He could have bowed to the pressure and changed his style when critics said it was the wrong approach. Instead, Tony chose to believe in himself and his methods, and was rewarded for his faith in his ideas. That's the message Tony Dungy has for others—always be true to yourself.

Quiet Strength: The Principles, Practices, and Priorities of a Winning Life, the memoir Tony wrote with Nathan Whitaker, became a bestseller when it was released shortly before the 2007 football season.

The Big Game

The Super Bowl is the most widely viewed professional sports contest in the United States. Among the other championships of popular professional sports—the World Series of Major League Baseball, the finals of the National Basketball Association, and the Stanley Cup Finals of the National Hockey League—the Super Bowl has the shortest history, dating back to 1967.

During the 1960s, there was not one major professional football association but two: the long-established National Football League (NFL) and the upstart American Football League (AFL). By the middle of that decade the rivalry between the two leagues had reached a fever pitch. Finally, in 1966, the two leagues agreed that they would merge into one league made up of two conferences.

The first Super Bowl was played between the NFL's Green Bay Packers and the AFL's Kansas City Chiefs at the Los Angeles Memorial Coliseum on January 15, 1967. The game was shown on two television networks, CBS and NBC, and was attended by 61,946 fans. By today's standards, total attendance was poor, as there were nearly 30,000 empty seats in the Coliseum.

Since that first Super Bowl, the contest has gone on to become one of the biggest sporting events in the world. It typically is the top-rated television program of the year. As a result, companies pay millions of dollars to buy 30 seconds of commercial time during the game's broadcast.

NFL commissioner Pete Rozelle hands the victory trophy to Green Bay head coach Vince Lombardi after the first Super Bowl, January 15, 1967.

African-American Coaches in the NFL

Seven and a half decades before Tony Dungy became the first African-American coach to win the Super Bowl, Frederick "Fritz" Douglass Pollard (1894–1986) became the first black head coach in professional football. Pollard was named co-coach of the Akron Pros in 1921 while also maintaining a spot as the team's running back. Along with Bobby Marshall (1880–1957), Pollard was one of two African Americans playing professional football at the time.

For nearly 70 years after Pollard made history, there were no other African-American head coaches in the NFL. Art Shell finally became the second when he was named head coach of the Oakland Raiders in 1989. However, there were only a handful of African-American head coaches and assistants throughout the 1990s.

The Fritz Pollard Alliance, a group of NFL minority coaches, scouts, and other individuals, was formed in 2003. Seeking to increase the presence of African-American coaches by creating more hiring opportunities, this group worked with the NFL to create the Diversity Committee. One of the committee's most important achievements was establishing the "Rooney Rule," named for Pittsburgh Steelers owner Dan Rooney. The rule stipulated that teams searching for a head coach must interview at least one minority candidate or be penalized.

Between 2002—the year before the Rooney Rule was adopted—and 2006, the number of African-American head coaches more than tripled.

Fritz Pollard, a pioneering African-American football player and coach, receives a plaque commemorating his accomplishments, 1954.

The War Heroes From Tuskegee

Before World War II, African Americans served in the military but were denied the best opportunities, given lower-level jobs, and often segregated from white soldiers. The success the Tuskegee Airmen had in key campaigns of World War II played an important role in putting an end to discrimination against black service members.

The U.S. military had refused to train African Americans as pilots before World War II. In 1941, various African-American groups led a successful fight to be allowed to fly. As a result, the military formed the 99th Pursuit Squadron, an all African-American flying unit based at Tuskegee Army Air Field in Alabama. The unit's members would become known as the Tuskegee Airmen.

The first five graduates completed training in 1942. By 1946, nearly 1,000 African-American pilots had graduated from Tuskegee. A total of 450 Tuskegee Airmen flew in North Africa and Italy during World War II. The 99th Squadron flew more than 200 combat missions, and its members earned many medals for bravery.

In recognition for their exemplary service, the Tuskegee Airmen received two Presidential Citations. In 1948, President Truman signed an executive order that ended segregation in the military.

A group of African-American fighter pilots attend a pre-mission briefing in Italy, March 1945.

Pioneer Quarterbacks

Hall of Fame running back Fritz Pollard became the first African-American quarterback in professional football when he briefly took the position for a few games in 1923. In 1953, Willie Thrower, a backup quarterback on the Chicago Bears, became the first African American to play the position in an NFL game since Pollard.

Pollard and Thrower's stints as quarterbacks were rare and brief, though. For decades, African-American college quarterbacks were converted to other positions when they were drafted into the NFL. During the 1970s, quarterback James Harris signaled a new era. He was the first African-American quarterback to start a playoff game, and the first to be named to the Pro Bowl.

In subsequent years, more black quarterbacks followed the leads of Pollard, Thrower, and Harris. In 1988, Doug Williams of the Washington Redskins became the first African-American quarterback to play in and win the Super Bowl. Warren Moon, who was signed by the Houston Oilers in 1984, went on to have a stellar career and become the first black quarterback of the modern era to be inducted into the Pro Football Hall of Fame. Today, African-American quarterbacks regularly start for teams throughout the NFL.

James Harris played 13 seasons in the NFL with the Buffalo Bills (1969–72), Los Angeles Rams (1973–76), and San Diego Chargers (1977–81). During his career, Harris threw 45 touchdown passes. Harris's best season came in 1974, when he appeared in the Pro Bowl and was named the game's Most Valuable Player.

A Champion Coach

When Chuck Noll became head coach of the Pittsburgh Steelers in 1969, it was hard to foresee the heights of success to which his team would climb. Before Noll, the Steelers hadn't won a championship during their 40 years in existence. However, by the time he left the team in 1991, the team had won four Super Bowls and nine AFC Central championships. They were considered one of the best franchises in the NFL.

A graduate of the University of Dayton, Noll was a guard and linebacker for the Cleveland Browns from 1953 to 1959. Before taking over in Pittsburgh, he was an assistant coach with the Los Angeles Chargers (which during Noll's tenure moved to San Diego) and the Baltimore Colts.

In Noll's first season as coach, the Steelers ended the year with a 1–13 record. However, over the next few years Noll quickly rebuilt the team by making a number of key selections in the NFL draft. In 1972 the Steelers won their first AFC Championship. They went on to win Super Bowls in 1975, 1976, 1979, and 1980, making Noll the only coach to lead a team to four Super Bowl victories.

Chuck Noll was named NFL Coach of the Year in 1989. When he retired in 1991, his career record stood at 209–156–1. Two years later, Noll was inducted into the Hall of Fame.

Chuck Noll became the first NFL coach to win four Super Bowls. During his career as a coach, he was known as a fair man who provided opportunities to talented African Americans.

Leading the Team

An NFL head coach implements his team's strategy by coordinating with a number of coaches. Two of those coaches, the defensive coordinator and the offensive coordinator, play pivotal roles in the team's success. Along with reporting directly to the head coach, the coordinators oversee a number of assistant coaches.

During training camp, the defensive coordinator will introduce the players to the strategy that will be used throughout the season. Typically, the defense will be adjusted for each game, based on that week's opponent. The defensive coordinator's assistants are typically in charge of one group of players. These assistants usually include a defensive line coach, a linebackers coach, and a secondary coach.

The offensive coordinator has similar responsibilities regarding his team's offense. The assistants who report to the offensive coordinator generally include the quarterbacks coach, the running backs coach, the tight ends coach, and the offensive line coach.

On game day, the level of a head coach's direction depends largely on his background working with the various team units. If a head coach is a former defensive coordinator, for instance, he may be more involved with directing the defense; if he has more experience leading offenses, he may even assume the role of calling plays, a duty otherwise reserved for the offensive coordinator.

The Legacy of Cover 2

Tony's Buccaneers became famous for playing a defensive scheme nicknamed "Tampa 2." According to Tony, it is really a variation of the Cover 2 defense he learned while playing with the Steelers.

Tampa 2 uses what is known as "zone coverage." In a zone defense, a player is responsible for covering a section of the field. This setup differs fundamentally from man-to-man defense, in which each player is assigned to cover a specific player on offense.

Tampa 2 starts with a defensive line made up of quick players who are able to put pressure on the quarterback. Setting up behind the defensive linemen, three linebackers and two cornerbacks cover the "short zones"—areas near the line of scrimmage. Behind these backs are positioned the two safeties, who protect the deep zones down the field. Each safety is responsible for half the field. During a passing play, a speedy middle linebacker must get back fast to help cover the middle of the field while the safeties handle the perimeters.

Players can easily learn Tampa 2. Its success depends on aggressiveness and effective execution. The strategy's major drawback is that it is vulnerable to the "big play": if the defense is facing a strong-armed quarterback with a quick release, the offense often has the option of completing a deep pass down the middle of the field.

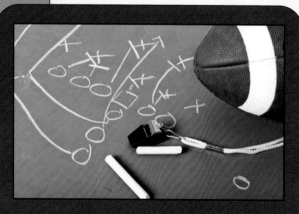

The Tampa 2 defensive scheme helped Tony Dungy turn the Buccaneers into a winning team.

A Family of Quarterbacks

The Indianapolis Colts' star quarterback, Peyton Manning, comes from a family of professional football players—all of them quarterbacks. Peyton's father, Archie Manning, was a quarterback with the New Orleans Saints, Houston Oilers, and Minnesota Vikings during the 1970s and early 1980s, and his younger brother, Eli Manning, is the quarterback for the New York Giants.

Peyton grew up hanging around NFL players and learning about the game from the pros. He attended the University of Tennessee, where he set numerous records for his school as well as for the Southeastern Conference. In 1997, he was named SEC Player of the Year and voted to the All-America First Team. A few seasons later, his number 16 was retired by Tennessee.

Peyton was the number-one overall draft pick in 1998 for the Indianapolis Colts. His records as a pro include most 4,000-yard passing seasons (8), most consecutive seasons with at least 25 touchdown passes (10), and highest passer rating for a season (2004). He was named MVP of the Super Bowl in 2007. A year later, Eli Manning won the very same award when he led the Giants to defeat the New England Patriots in the Super Bowl.

Eli, Archie, and Peyton Manning each achieved success as NFL quarterbacks.

CROSS-CURRENTS

A Tragic Problem

It is a sad fact that suicide is a common cause of death for many young people. According to the National Institute of Mental Health, suicide is the third most common cause of death among people aged 10–24. For every 100,000 deaths in the 15–19 age group, 8.2 are suicides; the rate of suicides for those aged 20–24 is 12.5 per 100,000 deaths.

It's hard to predict who will commit suicide, but some common risk factors include depression and other mental disorders, substance abuse, stressful life events, prior suicide attempts, and a family history of suicide.

Individuals who think someone may be suicidal should take immediate steps. First, do not leave the person alone. Then, inform him or her that you are going to get help. One of the best ways to find help is to call the National Suicide Lifeline (1-800-273-TALK). This lifeline is toll-free and service is available 24 hours a day, 7 days a week. A trained counselor can assist with an immediate crisis and also give referrals for local mental health services.

Lauren and Tony Dungy are escorted out of the Idlewild Baptist Church in Florida after attending their son's funeral. Eighteen-year-old James Dungy committed suicide on December 22, 2005.

A Rich Coaching Heritage

Sometimes the legacies of successful head coaches are extended by their assistant coaches, particularly in cases when those individuals become head coaches themselves. Often, a group of coaches linked together in this way is referred to as a "coaching tree."

Tony Dungy is part of several coaching trees. One such tree is made up of coaches who, like Tony, were taught by Chuck Noll of the Pittsburgh Steelers. Another tree is composed of the current head coaches who once worked under Tony. Coaches with defensive backgrounds dominate this second tree. Three of these individuals coached with Tony during his years with the Tampa Bay Buccaneers. Herman Edwards, who has worked as a head coach for the New York Jets and Kansas City Chiefs, was the Bucs' defensive backs coach. Lovie Smith, head coach of the Chicago Bears, was once the team's linebacker coach. Rod Marinelli, a head coach of the Detroit Lions, coached the Bucs' defensive line.

Tony Dungy has always given credit for his coaching style to Chuck Noll, who coached him both as a player and an assistant coach in Pittsburgh. Noll himself learned from legendary coach Paul Brown, whom he played for in Cleveland from 1953 to 1959.

Chronology

1955: Anthony Kevin Dungy is born to Wilbur and CleoMae Dungy on October 6 in Jackson, Michigan.

1970: Tony Dungy is recognized in the "Faces in the Crowd" section of *Sports Illustrated* for his athletic achievements as a junior high school student.

1976: Graduates from the University of Minnesota after setting numerous records as the Golden Gophers' quarterback.

1977: Signs a playing contract with the Pittsburgh Steelers, considered one of the best teams in National Football League history.

1979: Shortly after winning a Super Bowl with the Steelers, Tony is traded to the San Francisco 49ers.

1981: Officially retired as a player, Tony receives a job as the Steelers' defensive assistant coach; only 25 years old, he becomes the youngest assistant coach in the league.

1982: Marries Lauren Harris; becomes the Steelers' defensive backs coach.

1989: After leaving Pittsburgh, Tony becomes the Kansas City Chiefs' defensive backs coach.

1992: Tony moves from Kansas City to become the Minnesota Vikings' defensive coordinator.

1996: Hired as the head coach of the Tampa Bay Buccaneers.

1999: The Buccaneers continue to improve and they advance through the playoffs as far as the NFC championship game.

2002: Tony is fired by the Buccaneers and becomes head coach of the Indianapolis Colts.

2004: The Colts advance past the wild card round of the play-offs, then lose to the New England Patriots.

2005: The Colts again fail to advance past the divisional round of the playoffs; on December 22nd, Tony's son James commits suicide.

2006: The Colts finish the regular season first in their division with a 12–4 record.

2007: With the Colts' victory over the Chicago Bears in Super Bowl XLI, Tony becomes the first African-American head coach to win the Super Bowl; his memoir, *Quiet Strength* is released and becomes a bestseller.

2008: The Colts lose to the San Diego Chargers in the playoff divisional round; Tony announces that he will return to coach the Colts for the 2008 season.

Accomplishments/Awards

As College Player

All–Big Ten Second Team, 1975, 1976

Team's Most Valuable Player, 1975, 1976

Set University of Minnesota records in pass attempts, completions, passing yards, and touchdown passes

As Coach

Youngest assistant coach in the NFL

First head coach to defeat all 32 NFL teams in his career

35th coach in NFL history to win 100 games

Maxwell Football Club Pro Coach of the Year 1997, 2005

Sporting News NFL Coach of the Year, 2005

Honorary doctorate of Humane Letters, Indiana Wesleyan University, 2008

Indiana Football Hall of Fame, 2008

United States Sports Academy's Amos Alonzo Stagg Coaching Award, 2008

Charitable Work

Mentors for Life (founder)

Prison Crusade ministry

All Pro Dad

Appointed to President's Council on Service and Civic Participation, 2007

Chase Major Taylor Award (awarded for service to youth), 2007

Further Reading

Bell, Jarrett. "Dungy's Upbringing Was Super Solid." *USA Today* (January 30, 2007).

Dungy, Tony, with Nathan Whitaker. *Quiet Strength: The Principles, Practices, & Priorities of a Winning Life.* Carol Stream, Ill.: Tyndale House Publishers, 2007.

George, Thomas. "On Pro Football: Dungy and Buccaneers Keep Their Cool, and Keep on Winning." *New York Times* (December 14, 1999).

Goldberg, Dave. "Dungy's Quest Is for a Super Bowl Ring." Associated Press (December 9, 2006).

Hack, Damon. "Football: Manning and Dungy a Not-So-Odd Couple." *New York Times* (July 25, 2002).

MacCambridge, Michael. *America's Game: The Epic Story of How Pro Football Captured a Nation.* New York: Random House, 2004.

NFL Editors. *2008 NFL Record and Fact Book.* New York: Time Inc. Home Entertainment, 2008.

Internet Resources

http://www.coachdungy.com

Tony Dungy's Web site includes information about his books, his career, and his work with charitable organizations. A section also features a series of podcasts recorded by Tony.

http://www.colts.com

The official page of the Indianapolis Colts contains news and information about the Colts' players and staff. It also includes a calendar of Colts' events, photos, and audio and video clips.

http://espn.go.com/

The ESPN site contains statistics, rosters, schedules, and results for each NFL team. It also includes current articles and archives of past articles.

http://www.nfl.com/

The official page of the National Football League has news and information about every team, as well as links to other NFL sites. It also contains video clips and information about NFL Network programming.

http://www.profootballhof.com/

The Web site of the Pro Football Hall of Fame has biographies of every Hall of Famer, as well as historical information about pro football. It also includes video clips, photos, and a virtual tour of the Hall of Fame in Canton, Ohio.

http://sportsillustrated.cnn.com/

The *Sports Illustrated* Web site has statistics, rosters, schedules, and results for each team. Also featured on the site are current articles and a searchable archive of every issue in the magazine's history.

Glossary

demotion—a reduction to a lower rank or position.

discrimination—unfair treatment of a person or group, usually because of prejudice about race, ethnicity, age, gender, or religion.

execution—the process of fully carrying out what is required.

impulsive—inclined to act without thinking.

motivate—to provide someone a reason to act.

perimeters—boundaries or edges of an area.

physiology—the study of the life processes and functions of living things.

renowned—being widely acclaimed and highly honored.

segregate—to separate or set apart a group from the general population.

veteran—experienced through long service or practice.

vulnerable—unprotected from attack or damage.

Chapter Notes

p. 6: "This is why we marched . . ." Tony Dungy with Nathan Whitaker, *Quiet Strength* (Carol Stream, Ill.: Tyndale House Publishers, 2007), 292.

p. 10: "My line of work . . ." Dungy, *Quiet Strength*, 8.

p. 10: "And what do you benefit . . ." Quoted in Dungy, *Quiet Strength*, 291.

p. 13: "If you're going to be . . ." Dungy, *Quiet Strength,* 14.

p. 13: "Tony Dungy, 14, student president . . . " "Faces in the Crowd." *Sports Illustrated* (January 26, 1970), 61. http://vault.sportsillustrated.cnn.com/vault/article/magazine/MAG1083278/index.htm

p. 14: "What did you accomplish?" Jarrett Bell, "Dungy's Upbringing Was Super Solid." *USA Today* (January 30, 2007). http://www.usatoday.com/sports/football/nfl/colts/2007-01-29-dungy-cover_x.htm

p. 14: "I thought about it . . ." Ibid.

p. 20: "Champions don't beat themselves . . ." Dungy, *Quiet Strength*, 43.

p. 22: "Despite all the good things . . ." Dungy, *Quiet Strength,* 51.

p. 24: "Football is what you're doing . . ." Dungy, *Quiet Strength,* 57.

p. 27: "teachers more than tacticians . . ." Dungy, *Quiet Strength,* 96.

p. 28: "it didn't matter . . ." Dungy, *Quiet Strength,* 104.

p. 30: "A lot of times you take on . . ." Thomas George, "On Pro Football: Dungy and Buccaneers Keep Their Cool, and Keep on Winning." *New York Times* (December 14, 1999). http://query.nytimes.com/gst/fullpage.html?res =9806E7D81131F937A25751C1A96F958260

p. 33: "It's going to be good. . ." Damon Hack, "Football: Manning and Dungy a Not-So-Odd Couple." *New York Times* (July 25, 2002). http://query.nytimes.com/gst/ fullpage.html?res=9D04E6D91038F936A15754C0A9649 C8B63

p. 37: "Parents, hug your kids . . ." Dungy, *Quiet Strength,* 254.

p. 37: "Continue being who you are . . ." Dungy, *Quiet Strength,* 255.

p. 41: "Tomorrow night, there is . . ." Dungy, *Quiet Strength,* 290.

Index

Numbers in **bold italics** refer to captions.

Photo Credits

About the Author

BRADY CARLISLE is a freelance writer who lives in New York City. She writes educational material, and also writes about film and politics.